Rugrats Blast Off!

By Stephanie St. Pierre
Illustrated by George Ulrich

Little Simon/Nickelodeon
A Simon Spotlight Book

Based on the TV series RUGRATS® created by Klasky/Csupo Inc.
and Paul Germain as seen on NICKELODEON®

Simon Spotlight
An imprint of Simon & Schuster
Children's Publishing Division
1230 Avenue of the Americas
New York, New York 10020

Designed by David Turner
The text of this book was set in Century Expanded.
The illustrations were done in watercolor.

Manufactured in the United States of America
10 9 8 7 6
Library of Congress Catalog Card Number 96-80104
ISBN 0-689-81275-2

The Pickles were getting ready to drive to the country.

"This trip is gonna be lots of fun," said Tommy.

"I don't know," said Chuckie. "Riding in the car always gives me a tummy ache."

"Maybe if we play a game you'll feel better," said Tommy. "I gotta idea! We'll be astronauts going on a trip to the moon."

"That's not a half-bad idea," said Chuckie. "But we need some space stuff."

"Let's look in the toy bag," said Tommy. He found a big red rattle. "A perfect laser-blaster," he said. He also found some buckets.

Tommy's mom, Didi, put Tommy and Chuckie in the car. Everything was almost ready.

"Hi, Angelica," Tommy said.

Angelica glared at him. Then she stared at Chuckie. "Hey, how come you babies are wearing buckets on your heads?" she asked suspiciously.

"They're space helmets," said Tommy.

"We're going to the moon," said Chuckie.

"What do you mean we're going to the moon?" Angelica shouted at Chuckie. "We're just going on a stupid trip, stuck in these dumb car seats for hours and hours and hours. I'm already so bored I wanna scream."

“But that’s just it, Angelica,” explained Tommy. “If we make it into a game, we won’t get bored. You can play, too.”

Chuckie held out another bucket toward Angelica. She grabbed the bucket and glared at Chuckie. “Well, I guess I could play your silly game,” she said as she stuck a bucket on her head. “But *I* will be the Supreme Commander, of course. Start the countdown!”

“Five, four, three, two, one—,” Chuckie and Tommy counted.

“Wait a minute,” Angelica interrupted. “You’re supposed to start with ten!”

“We only know how to count down from five,” Tommy said.

“Argh! You babies can’t do anything right. Blast off!” shouted Angelica.

Angelica, Supreme Commander of the mission, gave orders to her crew. Moon Man 1, Tommy, was the pilot. Moon Man 2, Chuckie, was the navigator.

"Moon Man 2, look at the map and tell Moon Man 1 how to steer the spaceship," said Angelica. "Hey, watch out for that comet!"

"Phew! That was close," said Chuckie. He looked at his map. "Take a left at the Milky Way and watch out for the Sun."

"Wow! Look at that," said Tommy. "It's Spike, taking a space walk around a satellite."

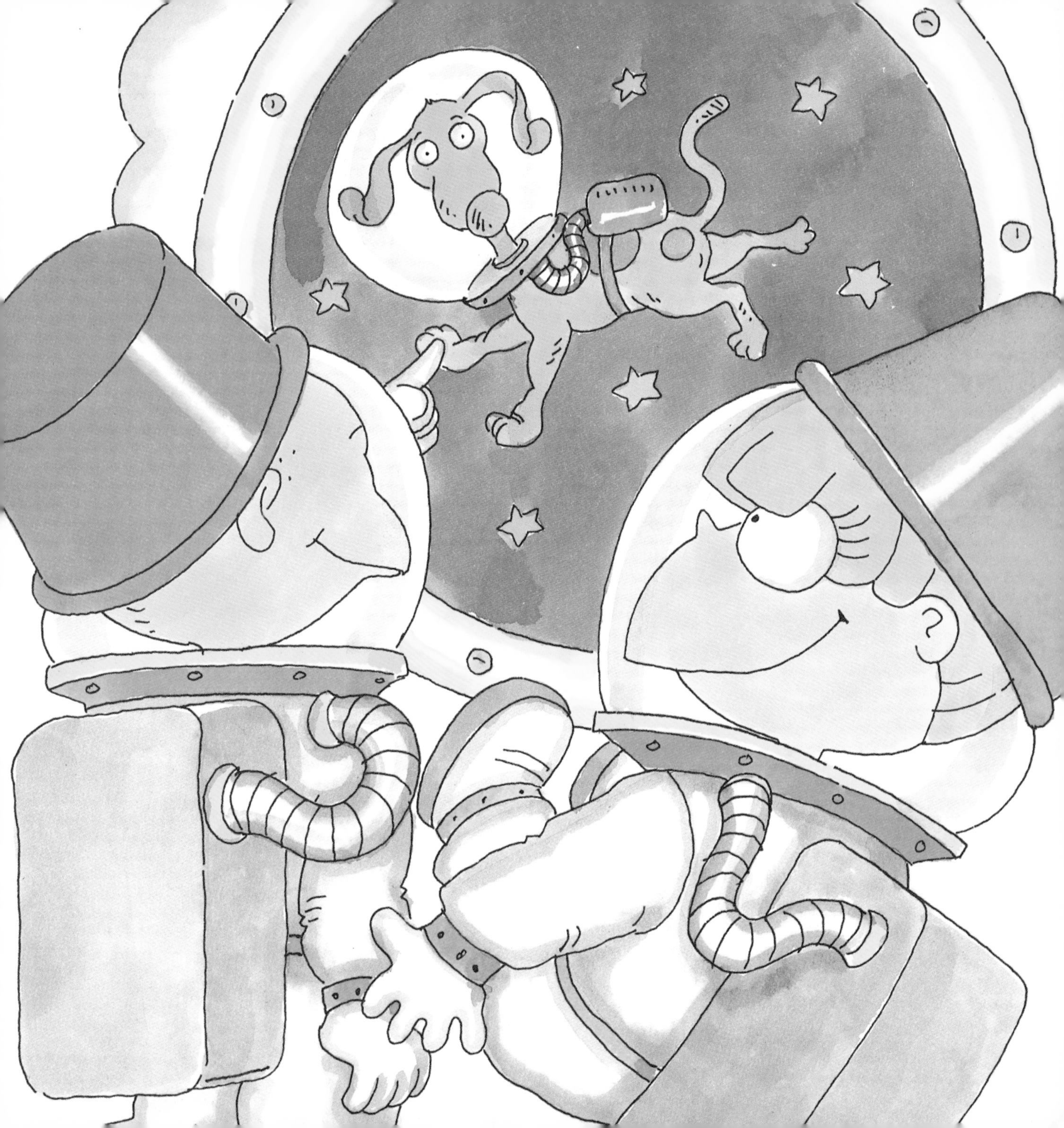

"Moon Man 1 to Moon Man 2, sounds like a message is coming in from Earth Station."

"Gee, Stu, that looks like a nice place to stop for a picnic," said Didi.

Stu pulled into the Scenic Overlook Rest Stop. "Everybody out!" he said as he turned off the car.

While Stu and Charles Sr. got the picnic things, Didi helped the kids out of the car. "You can play in the sand while we get dinner ready," she said as she set them down at the edge of a large sandpit.

"Shall we explore the asteroid, Commander?" asked Tommy.

Angelica, Tommy, and Chuckie surveyed the strange terrain. It was a wasteland as far as the eye could see, just miles and miles of hot, dry sand beneath a purple sky.

"Look! A volcano," said Tommy.

"Let's go," said Angelica. "But keep your blasters ready. We don't know what we might find out there."

"I wonder if there are any aliens here," said Tommy.

“Over there!” cried Chuckie. He pointed to the other side of the asteroid.

“It looks like another spaceship,” said Tommy. “But I don’t see any signs of life. I wonder where—”

“Grrrr . . . rah!” screamed something coming up the volcano behind them.

“As Supreme Commander, I order you to protect me,” said Angelica. She pushed past Tommy and Chuckie. “Whoa!”

Suddenly she was slipping down the other side of the volcano. Tommy and Chuckie were right behind her.

"Back to the ship! Back to the ship!" called the Supreme Commander.

Moon Man 1 and Moon Man 2 followed their leader as fast as they could, crawling through the open door of their spaceship back into their seats.

"We made it," gasped Chuckie.

They finally caught their breath. Tommy, Chuckie, and Angelica sat in their seats and looked around.

"Does anybody else notice that things seem a little weird?" asked Tommy.

"What do you mean?" asked Chuckie. "My bottle is just where I left it." He held the bottle up to drink but stopped suddenly.

"What's wrong, Chuckie?" asked Tommy.

"The last time I saw this it was a ducky bottle with chocolate milk. Now it's a kitty bottle and it's got some kind of weird-looking juice in it!" said Chuckie.

"Oh, no!" cried Angelica. "We must be lost in the wrong dimension. Look! I left Cynthia in my seat, but now there's a dinosaur!"

Suddenly two giant creatures poked their faces toward the kids.
“Aliens!” screamed Angelica, Tommy, and Chuckie. “Wahhhhhhhhh!”

The aliens stared at them for a moment.

"Whoa there," said a friendly voice. "Just settle down. I think somebody is looking for you."

Just then Tommy heard his mommy calling.

"Over here," one of the aliens called back.

Then Didi was there, peering into the van, too. "Tommy, Angelica, Chuckie—thank goodness!" she said.

"Gosh," Didi said to the aliens. "I guess they got confused because our vans look so much alike. Are these three babies yours?"

"They sure are," said the man.

The parents swapped kids, then sat down for a picnic. "Now let's eat before it gets dark," said Didi. Chuckie, Tommy, and Angelica looked around and were glad to be back on planet Earth, in the right dimension, too.

Soon they were back on the road.

"Are we still going to the Moon?" Angelica asked.

"Look! There it is. It's following us," said Chuckie.

Tommy yawned. "I'm too tired to fly to the Moon now. Maybe tomorrow." He looked out the window at the big round shiny white face in the dark sky. "Good night, Moon," he said, then he drifted off to sleep.